The Best Day Ever Savannah

written by Ellen Giordano

illustrated by Liz Beatty

Ordering Information:
Quantity sales. Special discounts are available on quantity purchases by corporations,
associations, and others. For details, contact the publisher at **hiltonheadkidsbooks.com.**

ISBN 978-1-7923-1000-3

For Meredith and Greg
and everyone who loves
adventure.

We are in Savannah for a wonderful day.
We hop on the Trolley to show us the way.

It will be the best day ever; there's so much to see.
Many adventures are waiting for you and me!

The Children's Museum is stop number one.
So much to discover, we're sure having fun!

The Railroad Museum is next on our list.
Locomotives and cabooses, we cannot resist.

Next to the home of a lady you may know,
She started the Girl Scouts, Juliette Gordon Low.

We are hungry for lunch,
to Mrs. Wilkes' Dining Room we head,

For lots of fried chicken, collard greens,
and rice that is red.

On to Forsyth Park, to the fountain we race.
We get our picture taken in this beautiful place.

We stop by Leopold's Ice Cream
on East Broughton Street,

For a double scoop of our favorite
ice-cream treat.

To Telfair Square and The Jepson Center we go,
To create art projects at the Drop-in Studio.

At Ellis Square, we find fountains for splashing.

We make new friends and do lots of laughing.

River Street is next, so many boats to see,
As they cruise down the river past you and me.

We go searching for something delicious to eat.
The candy stores here are loaded with sweets!

On to the Savannah Belles Ferry,
a ride we adore.

We see the Waving Girl Statue
standing on the shore.

The First African Baptist Church
is a place we must see.

We learn about the Underground Railroad,
and lots of history.

It's our last Trolley ride; we are ready to rest.
Our day in Savannah was simply the best.

Our time here was short, there's still much to do,
We're planning our next visit, we hope you are too!

Now It's Your Turn!

Savannah's a great place to learn and have fun.
Mark all the things you have seen and done.

BELLES FERRY ○

✓ WE HAD FUN!

○ 1ST AFRICAN BAPTIST CHURCH

CANDY SHOPS ○

○ ELLIS SQUARE

RIVER STREET ○

WAVING GIRL STATUE ○

○ LEOPOLD'S ICE CREAM

○ TROLLEY

○ JEPSEN CENTER

○ JULIETTE GORDON LOW BIRTHPLACE

○ CHILDREN'S MUSEUM

○ RAILROAD MUSEUM

MRS. WILKES ○

○ FORSYTH PARK

SAVANNAH

Share photos of your adventures with us on Facebook and Instagram!

  @bestdayeversavannah